TWEETY'S HIGH-FLYING ADVENTURE ™

Based on the screenplay by Tom Minton and Tim Cahill & Julie McNally

Adapted by Sarah Heller

WORLDWIDE PUBLISHING ™

SCHOLASTIC INC.

New York   Toronto   London   Auckland   Sydney
Mexico City   New Delhi   Hong Kong

No part of this publication may be reproduced in whole or in part, or stored in a retrieval system, or transmitted in any form or by any means, electronic, mechanical, photocopying, recording, or otherwise, without written permission of the publisher. For information regarding permission, write to Scholastic Inc., 555 Broadway, New York, NY 10012.

ISBN 0-439-20281-7

Copyright © 2000 by Warner Bros.
LOONEY TUNES characters, names and all related indicia
are trademarks of Warner Bros. © 2000.
All rights reserved.
Published by Scholastic Inc.

12 11 10 9 8 7 6 5 4 3 2 1   0 1 2 3 4 5 6/0

Printed in the U.S.A.

First Scholastic printing, September 2000

Illustrated by Ethan Summer
Designed by Keirsten Geise

"That bad ol' puddy tat," said Tweety. Sylvester the cat is always chasing the little yellow bird.

Tweety is very smart, and Sylvester cannot catch him. But Sylvester will never stop trying!

3

Tweety flew to his owner, dear old Granny. She was listening to a grouchy man named Colonel Rimfire. He was saying that cats were the smartest creatures on earth.

"Tweety is smarter than any cat," said Granny. "I will bet you that Tweety can fly around the world in eighty days. He can get the paw prints of eighty cats."

"Ha!" said Colonel Rimfire. No bird could fly that fast. "I will bet my entire fortune on it," said the colonel.

"Oooh! For Granny I will do it!" said Tweety.

Granny gave Tweety a special "Royal Passport." It had pages for lots of cat paw prints. Tweety was excited. He was going to fly around the world and be back by December 21 with eighty paw prints. Everyone cheered as he flew away.

Everyone except Sylvester.

Tweety's first stop was Paris, France. Sylvester was waiting.

"No time to stop and chat, puddy tat," said Tweety as he flew by Sylvester. Tweety was already busy – he was being chased by Penelope the cat.

Sylvester wanted Tweety for himself. "Nobody eats that bird but me, mademoiselle," said Sylvester.

While Sylvester fought with Penelope, Tweety got his passport stamped.

Pepe Le Pew broke up the catfight. Some cream had spilled on Penelope and Sylvester. Now they looked like skunks.

While the cats were confused, Tweety flew to Penelope.

"Tanks for the paw print," said Tweety. "Dat's one down!"

Tweety popped a piece of bubble gum into his mouth. He blew a big bubble and floated all the way to Venice, Italy.

"Oh, boy! Italian food!" cried Tweety. He was hungry.

"I'll have birdseed with your best spaghetti sauce," Tweety told the waiter. He ate and ate. Soon he was as round as a ball.

Now Tweety was too heavy to fly. He decided to take a boat ride. The Italian puddy tats wanted to join him. Tweety counted the cats as they jumped aboard. "Five, ten, fifteen – ulp!"

Tweety had an idea. He took a deep breath and rolled fast. He looked just like a bowling ball. The cats were the pins. Strike! Tweety hit them all.

The cats fell into the water. It was easy to get paw prints as the cats reached up to grab the wall.

"Whee!" said Tweety and he rolled away.

Tweety's next stop was in the Sahara desert in Egypt. But Sylvester was waiting for him. "There's my little desert snack," said the cat, licking his lips.

Sylvester dressed up like a mummy to trick Tweety, but some real cat-mummies got Sylvester instead. When Tweety flew away, mummy paw prints filled the pages of his passport.

"Dem's a lot of old puddy tats!" said Tweety.

Next Tweety flew to Tibet, a country in the Far East. He was surprised to see cats in robes. They were praying to a statue that looked just like Tweety.

Suddenly, Tweety noticed that the cats were standing around a small yellow canary!

"Omigosh!" cried Tweety. "Dose puddy tats are about to hurt a little bird!"

Tweety had to do something. He dove into the snow. His body rolled into a snowball. The snowball got bigger and faster as Tweety tumbled down the hill.

Crash! Tweety landed in the circle of cats. He saved the little bird. Her name was Aoogah.

"O great one!" bowed the cats. They thought Tweety was their god. "We will do anything you say."

Tweety was happy they said that. "Now write dis down," he ordered the cats. "You must never hurt another bird."

Aoogah hugged Tweety for saving her life.

"Aaaoooogah!" she cried happily. Tweety loved her loud birdcall.

"Do you want to fly with me?" Tweety asked her.

Aoogah was excited about the trip. She helped Tweety get more paw prints and they flew away.

DuBOIS

The two friends made many stops. First they saw the Great Wall of China. Then they were blown way off course to Mexico.

"Dat was one big gust of wind," said Tweety. Then they were blown all the way to South America.

"Enough of dis backwards business!" said Tweety. He and Aoogah held the passport and used it as a sail. Now they were back on track.

Next stop: Japan.

"Hurry up, Aoogah!" called Tweety. "There goes our boat to America!"

As Tweety and Aoogah rested their wings, Sylvester peeked onto the deck.

"I always heard there was lotsa food on these cruise ships," said the cat.

"Your food is downstairs," the ship's purser told Sylvester. "Now go get those mice."

Sylvester landed with a thud at the bottom of the stairs. In the kitchen, two little mice were eating some cheese.

Sylvester grinned. "I guess I'll have some mice snacks first."

Two mice named Hubie and Bertie were surprised to see a cat.
"Okay, here's what we're gonna do, Boit," said Hubie. He was
good at setting cat traps. He whispered his plan to Bertie.
Bertie let Sylvester chase him onto the deck.
"Whaoooo!" cried the cat. Hubie had dropped a bucket of
soapy water. Sylvester slid right over the side of the boat!

"Aww," said Tweety. "Da poor puddy wants to play with dose sharks, but his claws are all stuck!"

Tweety pulled out a crowbar. Into the water went Sylvester.

"Ooo . . . wook how fast dat puddy tat can swim," Tweety said, smiling.

"Help! Cat overboard!" cried Sylvester. He began to sink.

"Gee, I think Puddy is in weal twoble," said Tweety. He dove into the water and saved Sylvester.

"What I do for Warner Brothers." Tweety shrugged in disbelief. "Go figure!"

Suddenly a big wave came. Tweety, Sylvester, and Aoogah were washed onto a beach in Australia.

A huge wind blasted the sand on the Australian beach. It looked like a tornado! Tweety and Aoogah hid behind a small rock.

"It's a twister with really big teeth!" cried Sylvester. He tried to run away. But it was not a twister – it was the Tasmanian Devil. He grabbed Sylvester by the tail.

"Taz hungry," said the Tasmanian Devil.

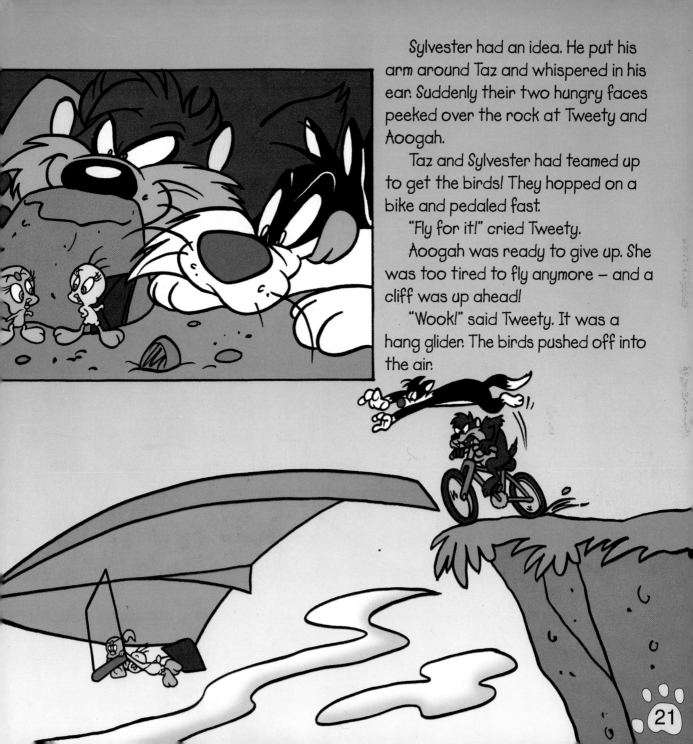

Sylvester had an idea. He put his arm around Taz and whispered in his ear. Suddenly their two hungry faces peeked over the rock at Tweety and Aoogah.

Taz and Sylvester had teamed up to get the birds! They hopped on a bike and pedaled fast.

"Fly for it!" cried Tweety.

Aoogah was ready to give up. She was too tired to fly anymore — and a cliff was up ahead!

"Wook!" said Tweety. It was a hang glider. The birds pushed off into the air.

Sylvester would not let his lunch get away that easily. He jumped onto the glider. The hang glider started to fall fast.

"So long, Puddy!" called the birds as they flapped their wings. They watched Sylvester fall and land on a windsurfer in the water.

Tweety and Aoogah landed on the windsurfer to enjoy the ride. Sylvester tried to catch them but he needed both hands to steer the windsurfer.

"Wooks wike we're gonna wide the waves all the way to San Francisco," chirped Tweety.

In the United States, Tweety and Aoogah flew to get more paw prints. However, it was not long before they heard a voice they knew.

"San Francisco tweets!" Sylvester said with a smile.

Tweety and Aoogah hopped on a skateboard just in time. It was a wild ride on the winding streets. Sylvester tried to catch the birds in a trolley car.

"Poor Puddy!" said Tweety. Sylvester had broken the steering wheel. The trolley car rode out of control through the streets of San Francisco.

While Sylvester was busy, Tweety and Aoogah took a train to Las Vegas. A sign said: COME CHECK OUR ODDS ON TWEETY'S 'ROUND-THE-WORLD TRIP. Tweety wanted to have a look. There was a big crowd of cats.

"I don't believe they want you to win," Aoogah whispered.

"And you won't!" shouted a cat.

It was Sylvester. He was leading the mob. As all of the cats gave chase, Aoogah surprised them with her loud birdcall: "AAAOOOOGAH!"

The two birds were able to escape. Tweety was happy to have such an alarming friend.

Tweety and Aoogah flew across the country. They stopped to get many paw prints. By the time they reached New York City, Tweety's passport was almost full.

"We're a whole day early," said Tweety.

So was Sylvester. Dressed as a hot dog vendor, the cat tried to stick Aoogah into a bun. Tweety outsmarted him again and the hot dog cart fell on top of Sylvester.

Poor unlucky Puddy!

"I'll get those birds!" pledged the cat. The newspaper gave him an idea.

It was time for Tweety to fly back to London. The little bird had a ticket on the Concorde, the fastest airplane in the world. He could win the bet a whole day early. But Tweety did not want to leave Aoogah. He did not want his adventure to end. "Give dis ticket to somebody who really needs it," Tweety told the airline lady. "I'm fwyin' home the old-fashioned way."

Tweety and Aoogah flew happily until the wind picked up. They were headed for a hurricane!

"Aooooogahh!" yelled Tweety. She was falling through the clouds!

Tweety called and searched. I'll never see my friend again, he thought sadly.

Then, suddenly, Tweety heard a loud call. Aoogah was alive!

"Lucky for me," said Aoogah. "Your passport floats."

When Aoogah and Tweety arrived in England they were cold and tired. The birds flew into a cafe to rest. It seemed empty, but someone was waiting in the shadows.

"I been followin' you so's I could get that passport!" cried a wicked thief.

Aoogah was scared. Whenever Aoogah got scared she screamed.

"AAAAOOOOOGAH!" Her cry shook the passport right out of the thief's pocket. Tweety grabbed it and flew.

Just then Sylvester ran into the cafe. He was hopping up and down with joy. In his paw was a "Wanted" poster of Tweety. By his side were three policemen.

"You, Tweety, are under arrest for stealing a Royal Passport!" said the police.

Sylvester grabbed the passport from Tweety's mouth.

"Wait! Look!" said Aoogah. There were two passports stuck together. As Aoogah pulled Tweety's away, Sylvester was left holding another. It had been in the thief's pocket. It was the real missing passport.

"Sorry we ever doubted you, old boy," the police told Tweety. "We'll take the cat to Scotland Yard!"

Now they were free to fly back to Granny, but Tweety hung his head.
"I blew it, Aoogah," Tweety sighed. "We're one day too late."

"No, we're not," said Aoogah. She pointed to a newspaper. The date was December 21. They were right on time!

"You mean we picked up a day crossing the international date line?" cried Tweety. "That means I can still win for Granny!"

Tweety and Aoogah lost no time flying to London.

"You did it!" cried Granny. She was so proud of Tweety. He had won the bet! Now she would get Colonel Rimfire's fortune. She was planning to spend the money to save a children's park.

"Not yet!" called Colonel Rimfire. "There are only seventy-nine paw prints in this passport."

Tweety could not believe it. He had forgotten Sylvester!

With a quick dash out the window Tweety saw what he needed. The police were outside with Sylvester. Finally, Tweety got his last paw print.

"Now I won the bet," said Tweety. "Tanks to dat bad ol' puddy tat!"

Tweety smiled happily at Aoogah. "And tanks to a special friend!" Tweety added with a wink.